BLACKBERRY FARM

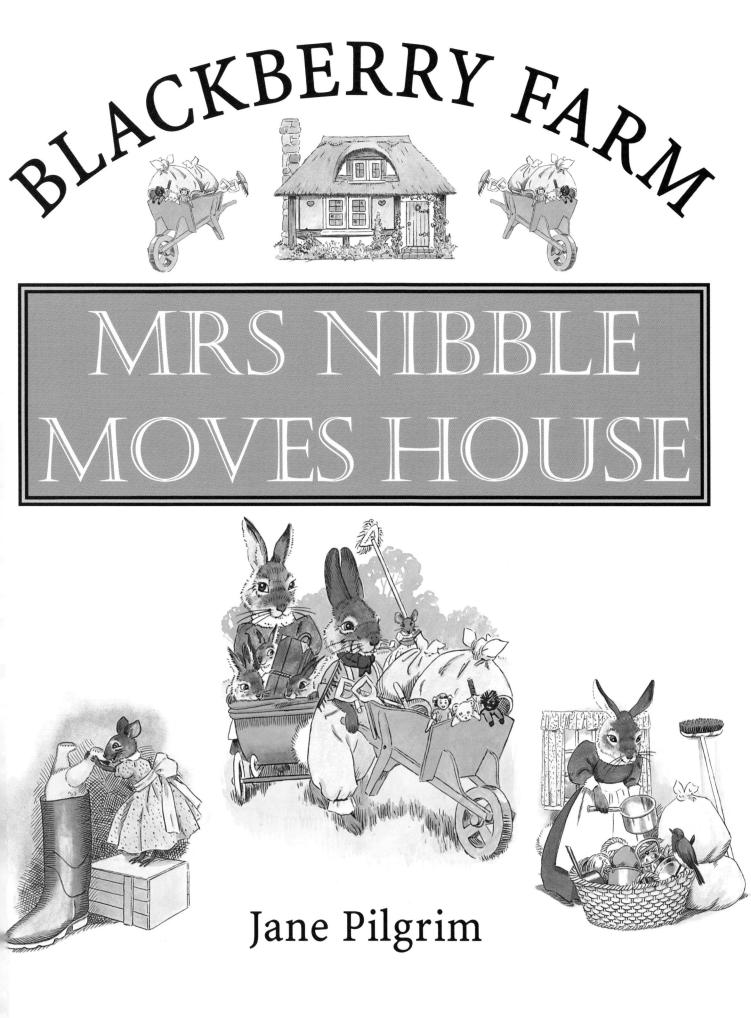

MRS NIBBLE MOVES HOUSE

Jane Pilgrim

This edition first published in the United Kingdom in 2000 by
Brockhampton Press
20 Bloomsbury Street
London WC1B 3QA
a member of the Caxton Publishing Group

Designed and Produced for Brockhampton Press by
Open Door Limited
80 High Street, Colsterworth, Lincolnshire, NG33 5JA

Illustrator: F. Stocks May
Colour separation: GA Graphics Stamford

Title: BLACKBERRY FARM, Mrs Nibble Moves House
ISBN: 1-84186-046-8

MRS NIBBLE MOVES HOUSE

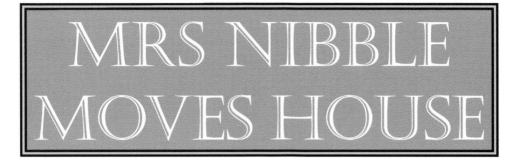

Jane Pilgrim

Illustrated by F. Stocks May

BROCKHAMPTON PRESS

Mrs Nibble lived with her three children, Rosy, Posy and Christopher, in a cosy little house in the field beside Blackberry Farm. Mr Nibble lived with them when he could, but he was a very busy rabbit and did a lot of work in the burrows on the other side of the village.

One day Mr Nibble came home at dinner time in a state of great excitement. "My dear," he said to his wife, "I have found a new house much nearer my work. We will move there this evening."

Mrs Nibble was very, very happy. "Now we shall be together all the time and when Christopher is older he can begin to help you with the work." And she called the children in to tell them the exciting news. Then began the great packing up for the move. Mr Nibble collected all the things he wanted from the garden and packed them in the wheelbarrow.

Mrs Nibble packed all the china and pots and pans in a big basket, and tied up the sheets and blankets in a big bundle. Joe Robin looked in while she was busy. "We are moving house to-day, Joe," she said. "Please would you ask Lucy Mouse to come and help me?" And Joe flew off to find Lucy.

"Of course I will come," Lucy
said when she heard of the great
move. And she collected her mop
and her brush and scuttled off to
help Mrs Nibble.

Mrs Nibble was very glad to see Lucy. "I have packed all the clothes," she said. "Please would you help the children to collect their toys and then we will clear up here before we go. I do want to leave it nice for the next people." And she explained to Lucy how nice it would be to live nearer to where Mr Nibble worked.

Lucy took Rosy, Posy and
Christopher round the garden to
find their toys and, when they had
got them all, they packed them in
the wheelbarrow beside Mr
Nibble's garden tools.

Then Lucy and Mrs Nibble put
the baby rabbits in the pram, put
the suitcase with all the clothes in
beside them and followed Mr
Nibble with his wheelbarrow across
the field towards the new house.

It was a very sweet little house
and Mrs Nibble was very pleased
with the roses which grew round
the front door and the neat little
flower beds under the windows.
"We will have a cup of tea before
we unpack," she said. And she
went into the kitchen to light the
fire and boil the kettle.

The kitchen was very empty, with no chairs and no table and no pretty china on the dresser, and Mrs Nibble felt a little sad. "But it will soon look just as nice as the other one when we get all our things in it," she said to herself. And she made an extra good pot of tea to cheer herself up.

They had a lovely picnic tea, sitting on the steps outside their new home. Then Mr Nibble went back with the wheelbarrow to fetch the furniture and Lucy Mouse went with him, so that she could give their old home a last sweep up.

Then Mrs Nibble and Lucy
Mouse made up the beds, while Mr
Nibble bathed the babies.
Suddenly there was a wail from
Christopher. "I can't find my
teddy. Teddy's gone. I want my
teddy." And he cried and cried, but
nobody could find his teddy
anywhere. Teddy had disappeared.

Lucy had one more look outside
the cottage. She looked inside the
watering-can and under the
flower-pots. But there was no
Teddy. Suddenly she thought of Mr
Nibble's wellington boots, and
there was Teddy right down inside
one of them. "I've found him!" she
cried and ran indoors with the
teddy in her arms.

Of course Christopher was happy, and everyone else was happy, and Mrs Nibble said that they must have just one more cup of tea and a biscuit, because Teddy had been found and because she thought it would be rather nice to have a little party the first evening in their new home.